Bird's New Shoes

Chris Riddell

For Quentin

Copyright ©1987 by Chris Riddell.
This special paperback edition first published in 2003 by Andersen Press Ltd.
The rights of Chris Riddell to be identified as the author and illustrator of this work
have been asserted by him in accordance with the Copyright, Designs and Patents Act, 1988.
First published in Great Britain in 1987 by Andersen Press Ltd. 20 Vauxhall Bridge Road, London SW1V 2SA.
Published in Australia by Random House Australia Pty., 20 Alfred Street, Milsons Point, Sydney, NSW 2061.
All rights reserved. Colour separated in Switzerland by Photolitho AG, Zürich.
Printed and bound in China.

10 9 8 7 6 5 4 3 2 1

British Library Cataloguing in Publication Data available.

ISBN 1 84270 252 1

This book has been printed on acid-free paper

Bird's New Shoes

Chris Riddell

Andersen Press • London

Bird decided to take his new shoes for a walk.
He met Rat.

Rat decided to go for a stroll in his new bow tie and shoes. He met Warthog.

"What a colourful new bow tie," said Warthog.
"It's the new fashion," said Rat.

Warthog went out for a breath of fresh air,
wearing his new hat, bow tie and shoes.
He met Buffalo.

"I say! What a splendid hat!" said Buffalo.
"All the best-dressed creatures have hats these days," answered Warthog.

Buffalo was grazing quietly, wearing his new waistcoat, hat, bow tie, and shoes when Goat came along.

"Excuse me, I couldn't help noticing your waistcoat. Is it new?" asked Goat.

"Oh yes, I'm a very fashionable buffalo," said Buffalo.

Just then Anteater rushed past.
  "I must get a cloak, everyone seems to be wearing them," he said.

"Yes, I've been meaning to get a cloak," said Buffalo.
"I'll get one too," added Goat.

Rabbit appeared. "Haven't you heard?" he said.
   "Rat says cloaks are old fashioned. He's wearing
a new pair of jeans."
   "We must get some," said Buffalo,
Goat and Anteater.

"Wait!" shouted Rat. "I've just seen Warthog - he's wearing sunglasses!"

Rat, Warthog, Buffalo, Goat, Anteater
and Rabbit were all having a quiet stroll.
They met Snake.

"I never go anywhere without my jeans," hissed Snake.

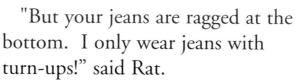

"But your jeans are ragged at the bottom. I only wear jeans with turn-ups!" said Rat.

"I never wear jeans with turn-ups!" said Warthog. "Bell bottoms are much more fashionable."

"Rubbish!" said Buffalo.
"Shorts are the very latest thing!"

"I don't think so," said Goat.

"Not baggy shorts anyway,"
said Anteater
    "Don't stick your nose in,"
said Rabbit.

Buffalo argued with Warthog, Warthog argued with Rat,
Goat bleated at Anteater, and Anteater stuck his nose in
the air at Rabbit. Snake sulked.

Just then Bird walked past.
   "Where are your shoes?" everyone cried.
   "Oh, I like to be different," said Bird with a smile.